lady bugs

music

stars

biking

Things that make me HAPPY

camp fires

birthdays

owls

dinosaurs

jellyfish

movies

Things that make me HAPPY

frogs

drawing

Things that make me HAPPY

narwhals

snow globe

fireflies

Things that make me HAPPY

trains

fuzzy socks

pizza

autumn

cozy sweater

For Adam, who makes me happy always.
—JB

For Amanda, who is my sunshine on a cloudy day,
my cheerleader when I'm feeling scared,
and the sister I never had but always wanted.
—HH

Sounds True
Boulder, CO 80306

Text © 2019 by Julie Berry
Illustrations © 2019 by Holly Hatam

Published 2019

Book design by Lisa Kerans

Printed in South Korea

Library of Congress Cataloging-in-Publication Data

Names: Berry, Julie, 1974- author. | Hatam, Holly, illustrator.
Title: Happy right now / by Julie Berry ; illustrated by Holly Hatam.
Description: Boulder, CO : Sounds True, 2019. |
Identifiers: LCCN 2019003092 (print) | LCCN 2019005093 (ebook) | ISBN
  9781683644200 (ebook) | ISBN 9781683643524 (hardback)
Subjects: LCSH: Happiness in children--Juvenile literature. |
  Happiness--Juvenile literature.
Classification: LCC BF723.H37 (ebook) | LCC BF723.H37 B47 2019 (print) | DDC
  155.4/19--dc23
LC record available at https://lccn.loc.gov/2019003092

10 9 8 7 6 5 4 3 2

Happy

RIGHT
NOW

JULIE BERRY

ILLUSTRATED BY
HOLLY HATAM

I'll be happy when
I get a puppy,
a unicorn,
an ice cream sundae,
and a castle with a friendly dragon.

Or,
I can be happy
right now.

I'll be happy when
the clock clicks the last second
of the school day,
on the last Friday
before vacation.

Or,
I can be happy
right now.

I'll be happy when
everyone adores me
for being brilliant,
brave, beautiful,
popular, and amazing.

Or, I can like me
right now,
and be happy
just as I am.

I'll be happy when
the worry monkey
gets off my back,
my chores are done,
and nobody's grumpy.

Or, I can feed the worry monkey a banana
and party with him on a jungle gym.
We'll both be happy right now.
Why not?

I'll be happy when
the rainstorm slows,
the icicles melt,
the clouds leave town,
and the sun says, "Come play!"

Or, I can be happy any day,
in mittens, in boots, or in soaking wet puddles.
Wetter is better anyway.

I'll be happy when
this sneezing stops.
No more sniffles and drips.
No coughs, no ick,
and I feel better.

Or, I can be cozy right now,
and snuggle down for a sleepy snooze.

And if it's up to me to choose,
    why lose time
        being gray,
            being blue?

All I need to do
    is be happy right now,
        whatever the day,
            whatever the weather.

Bunnies
Kindness
Unicorns
Magic
Happy Right Now
Dragons
Love ♥
Dreams
Diary

But . . .
But . . .
What about when
"happy right now"
is a no-can-do?
When the troubles and
sadness are much too much,
and feeling my feelings
is all I can do?

Like a long good-bye,

or a puffy-eyed cry,

or slow sorrows with no
good answer to "Why?"

Well, that's okay too.

I can breathe right now.
In is one.
Out is two.
Breathe again, fill my belly.
Let it flow out slowly.
Feel my body relax.
Let my bones turn to jelly.

Remember a now that was happy.
Breathe.

Borrow an old smile from a brighter day.
Breathe.

Know that happy will find me again soon.

Give a hug and get one.

Help somebody.

Learn something new.

Draw a picture, bake a cake,
talk it out, let it go.

Take a nap. Take two.

I'll be happy when
I'm hopeful,
cheerful,
helpful,
thankful.

Reaching for happy
until I can grab it.

No dragons required.

But I would like a rabbit.